Play with "i" and "g"

The Child's World®

Library of Congress Cataloging-in-Publication Data
Moncure, Jane Belk.
Play with "i" and "g" / by Jane Belk Moncure ; illustrated by Colin King.
p. cm.
Summary: A brief tale showing how "i" and "g" can be
combined with other letters to form simple words.
ISBN 1-56766-935-2 (Library bound)
[1. Alphabet.] I. King, Colin, ill. II. Title.
PZ7.M739 Pi 2001
[E]—dc21
00-010845

Play with "i" and "g"

Jane Belk Moncure

illustrated by Colin King

Starring the letters...

and

The publisher wishes to thank the letters "i" and "g."
Without them this book would not be possible.

This is little

This is little g.

and play.

What can we be?

This is little P.

May I play?

What can we three be?

Pig.

Play pig.

Do what a pig can do.

This is little

May I play?

What can we three be?

Wig.

Play with a wig!

What is that?

A wig on a pig!

A piggy-wiggy.

A wiggy-piggy.

This is little

May I play?

What can we three be?

Jig.

Dance a jig!

Dance a jig, pig.

Dance a jig. . .

pig in a wig!

What is that?

A pig. . .on a wig.

Get off the wig, pig.

Good-bye, wig.

Good-bye, pig.

Good-bye, jig.

and

also play with

b and **d**.

Can you?

ABOUT THE AUTHOR AND ILLUSTRATOR

Jane Belk Moncure began her writing career when she was in kindergarten. She has never stopped writing. Many of her children's stories and poems have been published, to the delight of young readers, including her son Jim, whose childhood experiences found their way into many of her books.

Mrs. Moncure's writing is based upon an active career in early childhood education. A recipient of an M.A. degree from Columbia University, Mrs. Moncure has taught and directed nursery, kindergarten, and primary grade programs in California, New York, Virginia, and North Carolina. As a former member of the faculties of Virginia Commonwealth University and the University of Richmond, she taught prospective teachers in early childhood education.

Mrs. Moncure has travelled extensively abroad, studying early childhood programs in the United Kingdom, The Netherlands, and Switzerland. She was the first president of the Virginia Association for Early Childhood Education and received its award for outstanding service to young children.

A resident of North Carolina, Mrs. Moncure is currently a full-time writer and educational consultant. She is married to Dr. James A. Moncure, former vice president of Elon College.

Colin King studied at the Royal College of Art, London. He started his freelance career as an illustrator, working for magazines and advertising agencies.

He began drawing pictures for children's books in 1976 and has illustrated over sixty titles to date.

Included in a wide variety of subjects are a best-selling children's encyclopedia and books about spies and detectives.

His books have been translated into several languages, including Japanese and Hebrew. He has four grown-up children and lives in Suffolk, England, with his wife, three dogs, and a cat.